Pig on a Swing

Written by Jenny Nimmo

Illustrated by Caroline Uff

Distributed by
Trafalgar Square
North Pomfret, Vermont 05053

Hodder
Children's
Books

A division of Hodder Headline Limited

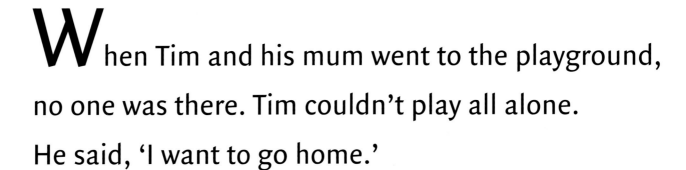

When Tim and his mum went to the playground, no one was there. Tim couldn't play all alone.

He said, 'I want to go home.'

'Wait,' said his mum, 'I think I can see – what can it be, sitting on a swing?'

Tim looked at the swings. What was there?

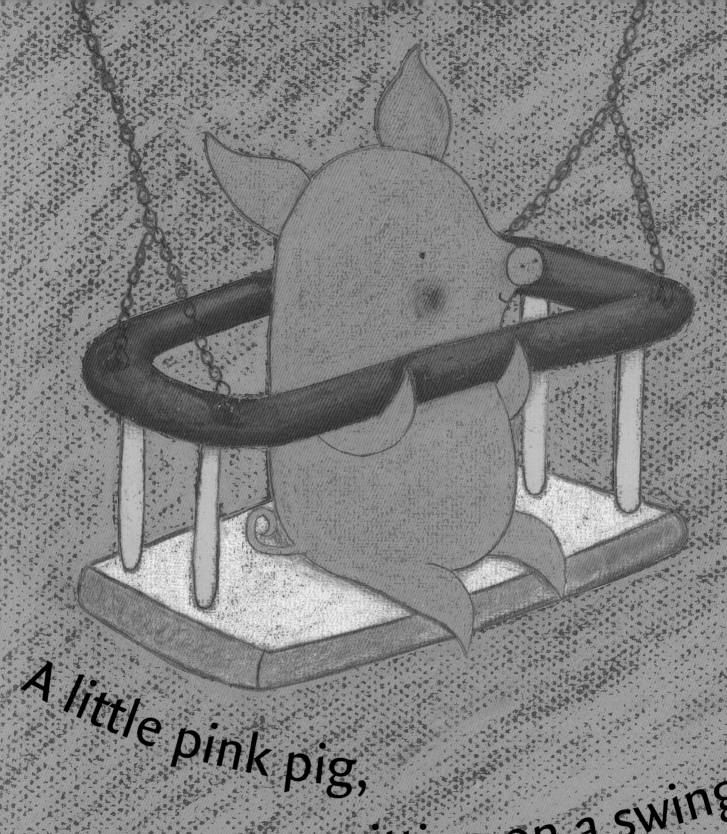

A little pink pig,

sitting on a swing.

Tim ran to the swings and sat beside pig.

He swung up high...

He swung down low...

He swung right into the bright blue sky.

And the pig swung beside him,
low,
high,
pig in the sky.

'**Whee!**' cried Tim. 'Look at me!'
Mum waved at Tim.
'**Oink!**' went the pig.
Mum waved to the pig.

Tim looked at the seesaw.
He couldn't bump up and
down by himself.

'Look again,' said his mum.
Something bumped on the seesaw.
What was there?

A kangaroo!

Tim sat on the seesaw.
The pig sat behind him and up they flew,
high, high, high.

Down they came...

...BUMP to the bottom.
'**Oooff!**' went Tim.
'**Oink!**' went the pig.
'**Bump!**' went the kangaroo.

Mum waved to them all.

Tim looked at the climbing frame.
He couldn't climb on his own.
'Look again,' said his mum.
Something growled on the climbing frame.
What was there?

A polar bear.

Tim ran to the climbing frame.
So did the pig and the kangaroo.

Tim climbed up high
and called, **'Yoo-hoo!'**

Then he swung down
low and went, **'Boo!'**

'**Oink!**' went the pig.

'**Bump!**' went the kangaroo.

'**Growl!**' went the bear.

Mum waved at everyone and then she sat down.
Tim wanted to slide. 'Look,' he said, 'there's something
squawking on the slide.'

'Yes,'
said
Mum.

'It's a
cockatoo.'

Tim climbed up the ladder.
The pig came after him, and then the kangaroo.
Next came the polar bear,
and last the cockatoo.

Up they went...

...high, high, high, high.

Down they went...

...WHOOOSH!

to the bottom.

'**Ow!**' went Tim.
'**Oink!**' went the pig.
'**Bump!**' went the kangaroo.
'**Growl!**' went the bear.
'**Squawk!**' went the cockatoo.
Mum waved at them all.

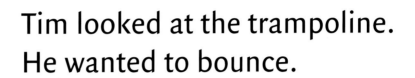

Tim looked at the trampoline.
He wanted to bounce.

'Come on,' he cried...

...'there's a skinny, brown hare thumping on the trampoline.'

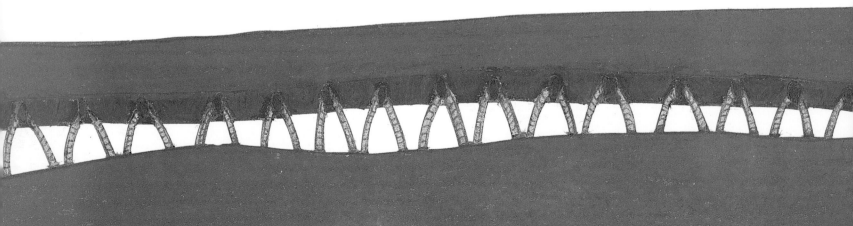

Tim jumped on the trampoline.
So did the pig and the kangaroo.
So did the bear and the cockatoo.

Up they bounced, high, high, high.

Down they came, BANG on their bottoms.

'Heee!' laughed Tim.

'Oink!' went the pig.

'Bump!' went the kangaroo.

'**Growl!**' went the bear.
'**Squawk!**' went the cockatoo.
'**Thump!**' went the hare.

They all lay together in a great, big heap.

Mum stood up.
'Where are you, Tim?'

'Here I am! I was under all the animals. Now I'm ready for my tea.'

Tim and his mum walked into the street.
The lights had come on and the evening was dark.

When Tim looked behind him,
   they were still there:
      the pig and the kangaroo,
         the bear and the cockatoo,
            and the skinny brown hare.

'Goodbye!' called Tim. 'Can we play tomorrow?'

Animal whispers stole through the dark.

'Oink!' went the pig.

'Bump!' went the kangaroo.

'Growl!' went the bear.

'Squawk!' went the cockatoo.

And the hare whispered, 'Yes!'